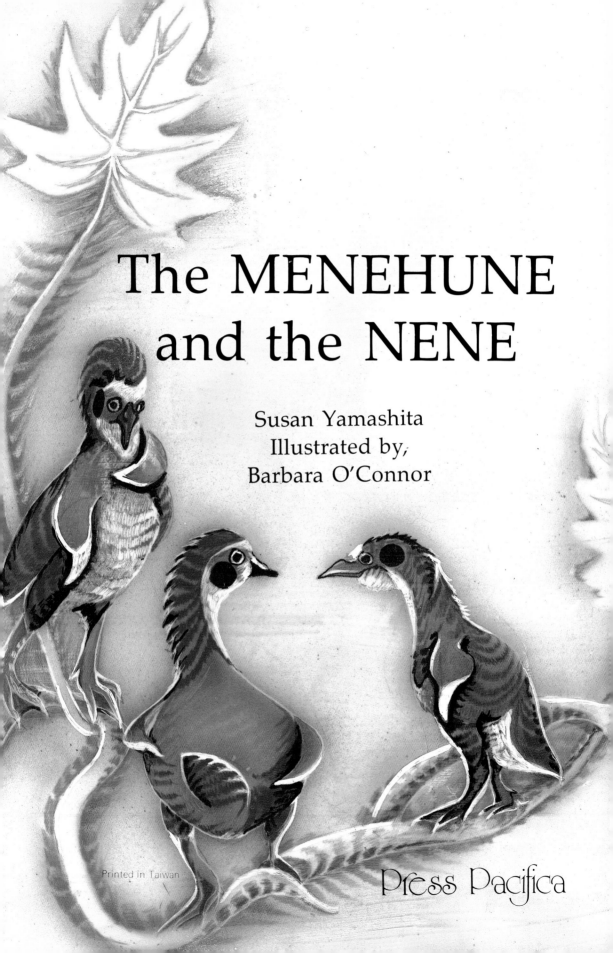

# The MENEHUNE and the NENE

Susan Yamashita
Illustrated by,
Barbara O'Connor

Printed in Taiwan

Press Pacifica

To my "little people,"
Tim, John, and Kate
And to my inspiration,
Cathy Holt

Copyright © (text)  Susan Yamashita 1984.
Copyright © (illustrations) Barbara O'Connor 1984.

Typesetting: Stats 'n Graphics, Honolulu, Hawaii
Printed in Taiwan

Available from: Press Pacifica, P.O. Box 47, Kailua, Hawaii 96734

Library of Congress Cataloging in Publication Data on  page 24.

# "THE *MENEHUNE* AND THE *NENE*"

Many, many people in the world believe in "the little people." In different places they are called elves, leprechans, trolls or gnomes. In Hawaii they are called *menehune*. Some *menehune* work hard all night digging ditches for taro fields but this is a story about a small group who decided long ago it was more fun to be up with the sun. These four tiny men lived near the top of the volcano, Mauna Loa, on the biggest Hawaiian island.

One day the *menehune* were gathering seeds when they discovered a treasure. It was a large, tan egg almost hidden in a tuft of grass. They looked around but it wasn't being guarded by bird or beast. Finders keepers!

They tugged and shoved the egg 'til it was out in the open. It looked perfectly delicious! The four *menehune* stomped their feet with joy and excitedly began to list ways to cook it.

"Wait a minute, you guys," the *menehune* Aka said. "First things first and the first thing here is to get it home." He turned. "Peke and Elema, you guys find us a wagon."

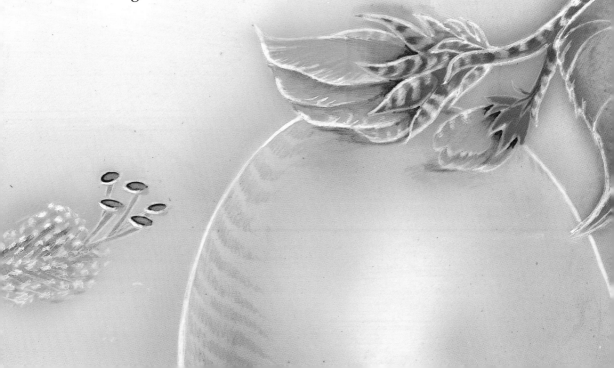

Peke and Elema trotted out of sight. Before long they reappeared dragging a leafy branch. It would do nicely as their wagon. Taking care not to be too rough with the egg so it wouldn't break open right on the spot, they half rolled and half lifted it onto the branch-wagon. Grabbing hold of the branch, they set out on the journey home.

It was a long trek. Across large, grassy areas, around big rocks and gnarled trees, past cracks in the ground with steam hissing, they dragged the branch. Across crater rim, around three huge, jagged chunks of old lava, past two scraggily bushes and a pool of water still overflowing from a rainstorm the week before, they dragged the branch-wagon.

The branch wore away and the egg was about to be scraped and bumped on the rough ground, when they arrived at their cave. First things having been done first, they arrived home with the egg.

Now the hard part. How to cook it? For two days Elema said he wanted it scrambled but Peke insisted they fry it. Aka sat with his arms crossed in front of him grunting "Poached." The fourth *menehune*, Puluke, saved the discussion from going three days.

"I've got it," he said. "Let's hard boil it and with one half make deviled egg and the other half egg salad."

Such excitement. The perfect solution! The *menehune* did not waste another minute. In record time twigs were gathered, a fire built and a pot of water put on to boil. Everything was ready. The four ran over to the spot they had hidden the egg. As they cleared away the under-brush, a faint tap, tap tapping could be heard. Aka bent over to listen.

"Well, we won't be eating this particular egg," he announced gloomily.

They all stared at the egg as the tapping grew louder. A tiny crack appeared circling the middle of the egg. More tapping. The crack widened. With a final push from within, the shell split open. Inside was a wet, scrawny baby goose called a *nene*. After pausing a few minutes to catch his breath, the *nene* struggled to his little feet and looked around. The first person he saw was Aka. Instantly the baby bird's eyes lit up.

"Peep," he cried as he ran over to Aka's side. A surprized Aka stepped back. The *nene* followed. Aka ran behind the other *menehune*. The *nene* followed, Aka dashed into the cave. Sure enough, the *nene* followed. There could be no doubt he thought Aka was his mother.

The weeks passed and it was always the same. Wherever Aka went the goose was sure to go. He was growing so fast he was soon a head and neck taller than the *menehune*. The cave was too small for him so his nights were spent outside in the grass or a rainpool.

There were other changes, too. The fuzzy down all over his body had been replaced by brown feathers; his head, neck and wings had black and white feathering. His "peep, peep" was becoming a "honk, honk." Yes, indeed, the *nene* was growing up.

"Not a minute too soon," declared Aka who often grumbled loudly that he couldn't wait 'til the goose was old enough to leave home.

"Aw, we kind of like having him around, Aka," said the others.

"Well, it ain't natural," Aka said. "He ought to be with one of his own kind."

One day Puluke asked "How can he leave home if he can't even fly?" he pointed out.

Aka scratched his head and stared into space.

"I guess we'll just have to teach him, he stated, confident of their ability to do so.

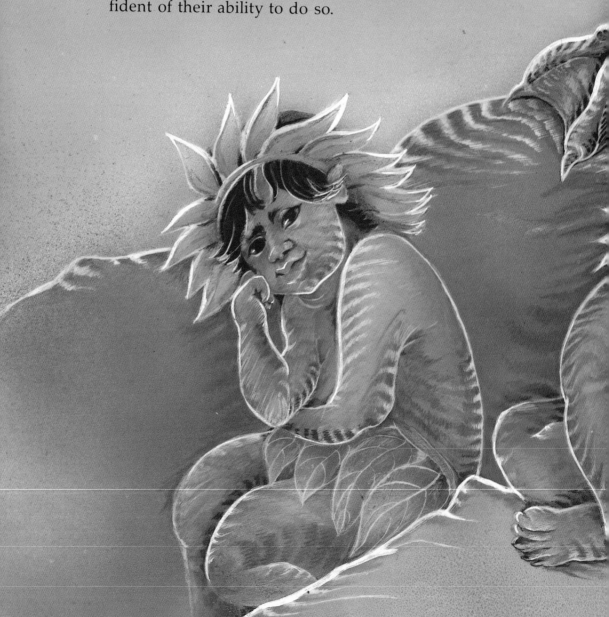

Flying lessons began that afternoon. They would chase the *nene* but he would only run. They would wildly flap their arms but he would only stretch and wave his wings. Nothing they could think of to get him into the air worked. Day in and day out for two weeks they tried. No luck. He didn't understand. Quite discouraged they gave up.

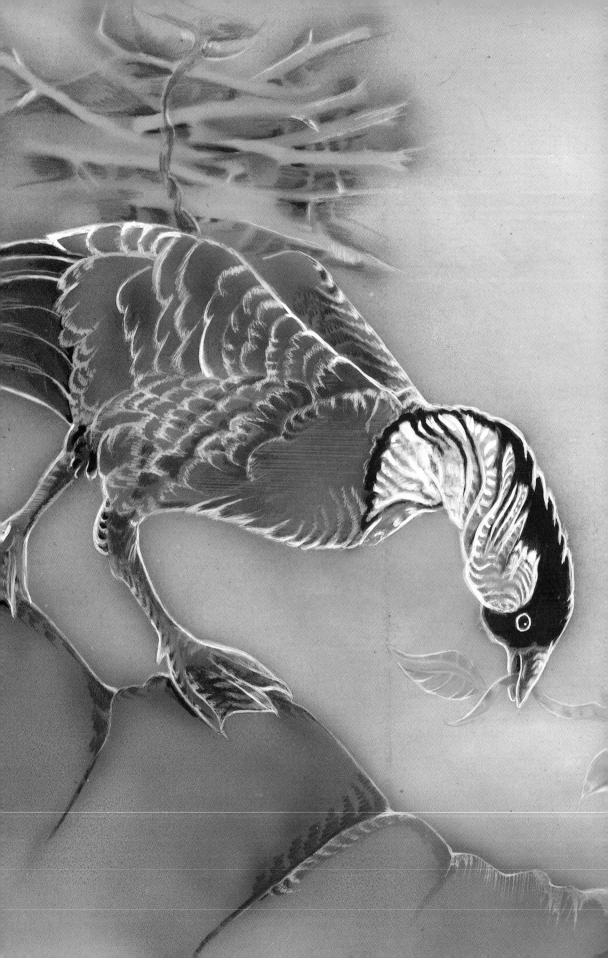

"Maybe he's too young," Elema offered.

"Naw," disagreed Puluke. "We've been watching *nenes* for too long not to know how big they have to be to fly."

"It's just that he thinks he's one of us *menehune*," said Peke. "We can't fly so he can't."

Aka looked balefully at the bird. "We're saddled with him forever."

"It's not as bad now as it was, Aka," said Puluke, the peace keeper. "He's been going off on his own some, wandering here, wandering there . . ." He stopped.

Aka wasn't listening. He had a gleam in his eye. "I've got an idea. Just figured it out when I said we're 'saddled forever'. We've been giving him the wrong lessons. Know what we're going to do?"

"No, what?" they asked suspiciously.

"Give him riding lessons!" Aka practically shouted with enthusiasm over his own genius.

"Riding lessons?" they hollered in disbelief.

"You bet. I'm not saying he'll have to carry us around much but we can sure use him to help us carry sticks and stuff. What do you say, guys?"

The little men looked at the *nene* and then at one another. "Well, OK, Aka, if you think it's alright and the bird doesn't care."

Aka started to train his goose. Within a few days the *nene* was carrying anything they asked him to. He even seemed proud of his job. As the days and weeks went by, he reached his full height and kept getting stronger and stronger. Even Aka changed. Nobody ever heard him complain about his goose.

One day just about sunrise, Mauna Loa rumbled awake as she does every year or so. For a couple of days the volcano shook with warning earthquakes. The *mene-hune* knew she would crack open again and spill her bubbling, red hot lava down the mountain. Most of the time she cracked far away from their cave and they weren't in danger but Mauna Loa was a short, fat mountain with lots of possibilities for cracking. It made them nervous. They stayed near their cave during times like these. They felt safer.

Suddenly on the third day, there was a huge tremor and the ground seemed to roll under their feet. Aka and Puluke climbed on a big rock to observe the volcano. It had happened. Far in the distance they could see smoke and orange tongues of lava leaping out of the earth. But the mountain was sloping away from them, and they knew they were safe for the time being.

The next morning there was another jolt. The four *menehune* climbed back on the rock and discovered to their dismay, there was a new crack with its dangerous, dancing lava. Already the molten, boiling fire-mud was oozing down the mountainside. They could see tufts of grass, bushes and trees catching fire as the lava slid along. As they watched, they knew they were squarely in the path of the flow.

"We can't run around it," Peke shouted. "It's too wide and our legs are too short."

"Maybe we can keep ahead of it!" Aka yelled.

The little band and their bird started jogging down the mountain (except the bird didn't jog - he waddled). It wasn't fast enough. Slowly but surely the lava came nearer. They could almost feel it getting hotter and hear the fire crackling in the underbrush.

"Our goose and us is cooked," Elema called out sadly.

"Well, the bird can't fly but he can run fast," shouted Aka. "Come on, guys."

Desperately everyone climbed on the *nene's* broad back. The goose was frightened by the heat and the unusual sounds and the panic in the tiny men. When all were in place and holding on for dear life, he started to run. As he ran the *nene* found that if he spread his wings out he wouldn't wobble too much with the extra weight on his back.

Down, down he ran. Without realizing it, the goose ran onto the outcropping of a huge, smooth boulder with no ground on the other side. It was a blind cliff. With his wings still stretched out for balance, the *nene* ran off the edge of the boulder. And a wonderful thing

happened. He was flying! The *menehune* could not believe their eyes. They shouted encouragement but the
big bird didn't need it. He was doing a beautiful job on
his first flight. And with passengers no less! Slowly the
*nene* began to beat his wings and headed far away from
the scary fire that had chased them.

Aka was so proud, he hugged his goose's neck. "And
to think," he shouted to the others, "we almost ate him
before he hatched! This bird's a hero!" He looked
down at the ground below.

"Now, Nene, let's find a safe new home for all of us."

Library of Congress Cataloging in Publication Data.

Yamashita, Susan.
    The menehune and the'nene.

    Summary: By the time four menehune decide what to
do with the nene egg they find, it hatches and the nene (goose)
soon grows large enough to save them from an erupting volcano.
    [1. Fairies—Fiction.  2. Hawaii—Fiction]   I. O'Connor,
Barbara, ill.   II. Title.
PZ7.Y918Me   1984              [E]              84-3290
ISBN 0-916630-42-0